A Lottie Lipton ADVENTURE

The Catacombs of Chaos

Dan Metcalf

ILLUSTRATED BY
Rachelle Panagarry

MINNEAPOLIS

For Jim and Barbara Metcalf

This Americanization of *The Catacombs of Chaos: A Lottie Lipton Adventure* is published by Darby Creek by arrangement with Bloomsbury Publishing Plc.

Darby Creek
A division of Lerner Publishing Group, Inc.
241 First Avenue North
Minneapolis, MN 55401 USA

For reading levels and more information, look up this title at www.lernerbooks.com.

Main body text set in Stempel Schneidler Std Roman 12/24.
Typeface provided by Adobe Systems.

Library of Congress Cataloging-in-Publication Data

The Cataloging-in-Publication Data for *The Catacombs of Chaos: A Lottie Lipton Adventure* is on file at the Library of Congress.
ISBN 978-1-5124-8183-9 (lib. bdg.)
ISBN 978-1-5124-8185-3 (pbk.)
ISBN 978-1-5124-8191-4 (EB pdf)

Manufactured in the United States of America
1-43162-32924-3/9/2017

Contents

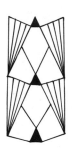

Chapter One
London, 1928

Lottie was hanging upside down reading the newspaper when she heard a yell from deep within the British Museum.

"For once, that scream definitely had nothing to do with me," she said to herself with a smug smile. Peculiar things tended to happen when Lottie was around. Objects came to life, treasures were discovered, and

Sir Trevelyan Taylor, the Head Curator of the British Museum, often yelled out and stomped his foot in frustration. Lottie unhooked her legs from the railing she was dangling from (she had been trying to find out if getting more blood to her brain made her any better at crosswords—it didn't) and hopped down. "I'd better go and investigate!" she announced to no one in particular.

Lottie grabbed her cardigan and her trusty detective's notebook and set off to find the source of the noise, which was bound to be coming from Sir Trevelyan Taylor's office. She paced through the corridors of the British Museum, where she had lived since she was four.

She passed ancient treasures, towering statues, and objects from thousands of years of world history.  She loved her home, especially living with her great uncle Bert in their messy flat on the grounds of the museum. She had a great time learning about history and the world from the library and practicing her detective skills (when all those peculiar things seemed to happen), which were about to come in handy.

"But it's impossible!" shouted Sir Trevelyan from inside his office. He sounded angry,

so Lottie wisely hung outside the door, jotting down what he said in her notebook. "I can't get a donation that large! Especially by tonight!"

Lottie continued scribbling until she heard the click of Sir Trevelyan's telephone receiver being placed back on its cradle. She quickly darted away from his office door, looking for a place to hide as she heard him stand and pace around his office.

"You may as well come in," called the curator's voice from the office. "I know you're out there."

Lottie gulped and poked her head around the door.

"H-how did you—"

"There's always a strange kind of silence when you're eavesdropping, Lottie Lipton," said Sir Trevelyan. "How much did you hear?"

Lottie entered the office properly and looked back at her notes.

"Um, something about a large donation?" she said. Sir Trevelyan sighed and stared out of his window.

"That was the chairman of the board of directors. They say they need an impossible amount of money to keep the museum running, or we'll have to close the whole place down."

Lottie gasped. "Does that mean you'd lose your job? And Uncle Bert?"

"Yes, and that useless caretaker too," sneered Sir Trevelyan. Lottie was going to protest about her friend Reg being called useless, but decided that now wasn't the time. "And you'd be thrown out of your quarters here. The whole museum would be shut down until the money could be raised."

Lottie bit her lip in worry. Sir Trevelyan, for all his unpleasantness, was a fighter. He never backed down from an argument or a challenge, but as Lottie looked at him she realized that today he looked different. He looked . . . defeated.

"I'll go tell Uncle Bert," she said, turning to leave. As she walked away from the curator's office, she realized that she would have to do the unthinkable.

She had to help Sir Trevelyan Taylor.

Lottie walked through the Ancient Rome department, where she found her great uncle Bert face down on the floor, his head pressed against the wooden floorboards.

"Are you all right, Uncle Bert?" she said, dashing over to him. "Did you fall?"

"No, no! Just, erm, resting . . ." he said, unconvincingly.

Lottie gave him a look that clearly said, "I don't believe you."

"Oh all right! I dropped a coin between the floorboards, and I was trying to see if I could get it out."

Lottie laughed. Uncle Bert, the Curator of Egyptology at the British Museum, had been left in charge of the Roman section for a few weeks while Cedric, the usual Curator of Roman Artifacts, was on an archaeological dig. He had only been gone for three days so far.

"Oh, Uncle! What did you drop? A penny? A nickel?"

"No, it's, eh, rather more valuable than that," said Uncle Bert with a blush. "A golden

Roman aureus. It was
two thousand years
old and part of the
Roman coin exhibit."

Lottie sighed and went
to get Reg, the tall caretaker
who lived on the grounds of the museum with
them. He came quickly, carrying a crowbar
and hammer instead of his usual mop and
bucket.

"Reg to the rescue!" he announced. "Where
did you drop it, butterfingers?"

"Are you sure that a crowbar is the best way
to go about this, Reg?" asked Lottie. "It seems
a bit . . . drastic."

"Don't worry, Miss Lottie! I'm an expert in these kind of situations."

Lottie suddenly realized that she hadn't yet told the two men about the important donation that Sir Trevelyan needed. But she just didn't know how to tell them. She didn't want to upset them, and she certainly didn't want to disturb Reg while he had a heavy hammer and sharp piece of metal in his hands.

After a minute or two of frantic hammering,

Reg lifted up the floorboard, and Lottie reached in to retrieve the coin.

"There it is!" she said, pulling out the shiny gold coin. Uncle Bert sighed with relief and reached out to take it. Lottie took a step back, out of Uncle Bert's reach, and said, "I think I should take care of this, don't you, Uncle Bert? I'll keep it safe."

"Oh, for goodness' sake! I'm not *that* clumsy! I'm perfectly capable of—"

THUD!

Uncle Bert fell to the floor as he accidentally stepped into the hole in the floorboards.

"You were saying?" smiled Reg. He helped Uncle Bert up, pulling his foot out from the hole. As soon as Uncle Bert had moved out of the way, Lottie noticed something under the floorboards.

She peered inside. "Reg, can you lift up the rest of the floorboards? I'm sure I can see something else down there."

After some more hammering, Reg had cleared a hole in the floorboards the size of a door.

"Lottie, what's the meaning of this, I—" Uncle Bert paused as he looked down to the see what Lottie had glimpsed. "Well, goodness me!"

Under the wooden floorboards was a stone floor with strange symbols carved on it.

"Wow!" said Lottie. "It's a message! It has to be!"

Delve deep to find the hoard

"Do you think so?" said Uncle Bert. "Goodness me. What can it mean?"

Lottie didn't have a clue, but she wasn't going to give up so easily. She stared at the markings, her brain working extra hard to figure out what the message could mean . . .

Can you figure
out the mysterious
markings?
Continue reading to
see if you're right.

"I still have absolutely no idea what I'm supposed to be looking at," complained Reg, peering over their shoulders. Uncle Bert moved aside to point at the markings while Lottie puzzled over the message. She racked her brain until she turned away in frustration.

"Oh . . . fiddlesticks!" shouted Lottie. She folded her arms and stared up to a high window in the room. It was tilted slightly, and a black cloud passed over the sun, allowing her to see a glimpse of a reflection. "Ooh! Oh!" she cried. "That's it!"

"Hmm? What's 'it,' my dear? I say, steady on . . ." Lottie had grabbed hold of Uncle

Bert's suit jacket and was reaching into his inside pocket to get the small hand mirror he used when he groomed his moustache. She found it and held it up in the air, looking at the reflection of the markings in it.

"It's mirror writing!" she called. "I can just make it out if I can hold this in the right spot! It says: *Delve deep to find the hoard.*"

Uncle Bert took the hand mirror, held it up so he could see the reflection, and confirmed that Lottie was right.

"*Hoard* means 'treasure,' doesn't it, Uncle Bert?" said Lottie, getting excited. Maybe she wouldn't have to tell them about the donation after all. "And *delve deep?* That means it must

be hidden under the ground! What are we waiting for? Let's get cracking!"

Chapter Two

Reg used the crowbar to pry up one of the slabs of stone. He lifted it up like it weighed nothing at all, but it made a heavy bang when it landed on the floor next to Lottie. *He's stronger than he looks*, she thought to herself. Underneath where the stone had been was a hole leading down into a dark space. Suddenly, Lottie wasn't so sure about her plan to go after the treasure. Uncle Bert noticed her hesitate.

"We could always wait, my dear," he said, placing a comforting hand on her shoulder. Lottie took a few deep breaths and shook her head.

"No. There's no time like the present," she said, thinking of Sir Trevelyan's warning. "Come on!"

Before the others could stop her, Lottie had dropped to the floor and jumped down the dark hole feetfirst.

"Lottie! Do you know how dangerous that is?" called Uncle Bert. He peered over the edge. "What's it like down there?"

There was a heart-stopping moment for Uncle Bert when Lottie didn't reply. Then:

"Dark!" came her voice. *"Really* dark. You may want to bring a lantern!"

When Reg and Uncle Bert joined Lottie, they brought with them Reg's old mining lamp that he had used in the trenches of the Great War.

"I think the tunnel leads down here," said Lottie, taking the lantern from Reg and

pointing it out in front of her. They were in a brick tunnel that seemed to go on for miles. Moisture glistened on the walls around them. With only the small lantern for light, they set off down the tunnel.

"What is this place?" muttered Reg.

"Goodness knows," said Uncle Bert. "London is littered with catacombs and subterranean spaces." He paused when he noticed Reg looking at him with a confused frown. "That's an underground passage. From the brickwork, I'd say this was built for one of the Victorian churches in the area."

"Fascinating," said Lottie. "What for?"

They walked along the passage a bit

farther, where Lottie found the answer to her question. On a ledge set into the wall lay an old wooden coffin.

"Storing the dead," said Uncle Bert. A shiver went down Lottie's spine.

"Ugh! How horrid," she said with disgust. "I came for treasure, not skeletons!"

Reg, who was bent double to fit his tall frame into the tunnel, walked along behind Lottie.

"What sort of treasure are we looking for?" he asked. "Diamonds? Rubies? Emeralds?"

"Gold," said Uncle Bert confidently. "A hoard of gold coins dating back to the year 60 AD."

"How on Earth do you know that?" asked Lottie.

"Because I think we are looking for the hoard of Boudicca," said Uncle Bert. "Legend has it that it is stored somewhere around—or under—London. Many have searched, but none have found it."

"Who's that, then?" asked Reg.

Uncle Bert smiled. He always loved the chance to show off his knowledge of history.

"Boudicca was the Queen of the Iceni, a tribe in the East of England. When her husband died, the Romans took over her lands. She led a rebellion against the Romans and marched to London with her army. It was poorly defended, and Boudicca and her army killed over seventy thousand people."

Lottie gulped.

"And the hoard is the gold they looted from the Romans?" she deduced. Uncle Bert nodded and pressed onward.

"Ooo, this is a strange one," he said as they came upon a heavy wooden door ahead of them. Uncle Bert tried the handle, but it was locked. He pressed his shoulder to the door and pushed with all his might, but even his bulky frame couldn't shift it.

"Ah well, we tried. Back to the museum for a cup of tea?" he said, attempting to push past Lottie. She stopped him with a glare.

"Uncle Bert, I came for treasure and I'm not leaving without it!" She squeezed past him to

get a closer look at the door. She held the lamp
close to the door. After further inspection, she
could see that the lock on the door was quite
unusual. There was a picture of some dials next
to it in an order she couldn't quite understand:

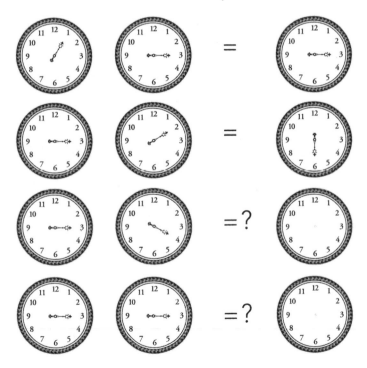

"Curiouser and curiouser . . ." Lottie muttered to herself. It was a saying from her favorite book, *Alice in Wonderland,* and it seemed to apply to her life more and more often lately.

"Another blinkin' code to crack," sighed Reg. "I knew I should've stayed up top. Now my brain's going to ache for the rest of the day!"

Uncle Bert leaned in to get a closer look.

"Come now, it can't be that difficult," he said. He looked closer and his smile faded. "We, um, must have to, er, put the thingies on the whatsits . . ."

Lottie rolled her eyes. She pointed to two arms that lay next to the clock faces.

"We have to put the arms on the faces, but pointing to the correct number."

"Yes, exactly! Just what I said!" laughed Uncle Bert. He frowned again and scratched at his ear, the way he always did when he was confused. "And, um, what are the correct numbers, my dear?"

Lottie looked at the dials and panicked.

"I . . . I . . . I don't know!"

Can you help Lottie? Read on to see if you're right!

Lottie's head whirled with numbers. She couldn't concentrate on the task—she was panicking too much! She handed the lamp to Reg and forced herself to close her eyes and hold her breath for five seconds. Then, breathing easily, she focused on the dials.

One plus three—that equals four, doesn't it? thought Lottie. *So why is the last dial pointing to three? Oh! Maybe it means one multiplied by three. That equals three! Okay, so the next line is three and two. If I add them it equals five, but if I multiply them, it equals . . . six! Which is the right answer! So, the next dials read—*

"Three and four. That equals twelve!" she

said aloud. She picked up the small hand and clicked it in place, turning it around until it pointed directly upward.

"Are you sure, Miss Lottie?" said Reg. "I'm no mathematician, but I thought three plus four equaled seven?"

Lottie shook her head and carried on.

"So the next is three and three," she said.

"Six!" said Uncle Bert with a cheery grin. Lottie ignored him and placed the hand on the face, pointing to nine. There was a whir and a click from inside the door mechanism, and Lottie tried the

handle. It turned easily, and Lottie stepped through . . .

Chapter Three

U gh!" called Lottie. "We should have brought rain boots!"

She stepped into the dark and felt the cold dampness rise through her shoes and socks as she sloshed through a puddle. Reg followed her with his lamp, illuminating the wet, muddy floor below them and the glistening dirt walls around them.

"This is a bit different, isn't it?" he remarked. "Reminds me of the time I mined tin in

Cornwall for a while."

"Reg, is there any job you *haven't* done?" said Lottie. She moved forward to allow Uncle Bert through the wooden door.

"Well, bless my soul!" he said, looking around with wonder. The walls surrounding them had been carved out of clay-like mud with shovels and axes, and the whole narrow tunnel was supported by thick wooden beams. It was very different to the Victorian brick tunnel they had just come through.

"It's like we've stepped back in time!" said Lottie. Uncle Bert inched forward, wary of the damp-looking wooden ceiling.

"In a way, we have," he said. "Around two

hundred years. I'd bet my bow tie that this is part of the first ever archaeological excavation of Roman London. The city had never been properly studied you see, and the first

chance they had to dig up the foundations of the buildings was when the whole lot burned to a crisp in the Great Fire of London."

Lottie stared at the humble tunnel with a new sense of awe. She began to look more closely at her surroundings and spotted some burn marks on the wooden beams where the builders had reused charred remains of a house from the surface.

"That dates this place to 1666!" she exclaimed. "That's even older than the museum."

"I'm not sure how safe these tunnels are," said Uncle Bert with a furrowed brow. "We should head back and get some helmets."

Reg prodded the walls. A small section crumbled away.

"Looks safe enough to me," he said with a shrug. "I'm happy to carry on."

Lottie thought of the promise of treasure, and of Sir Trevelyan and his warning that they might very soon lose their home.

"Me too," she said. "Come on, Uncle Bert, let's go."

"No! I said it is unsafe, so we should go back!" said Uncle Bert, putting his foot down (quite literally too, into a rather large puddle).

"Lighten up, Bertie!" said Reg. It turned out that this was exactly the wrong thing to say. If there was one thing Uncle Bert hated, it was being called "Bertie." His cheeks reddened as he stepped forward angrily toward Reg.

"That's Professor West to you, 'Reggie'! And I'll thank you to—"

SLAM!

A strange silence came over the tunnel as the three explorers looked back to the wooden door that they had come through moments ago. It had swung shut. As the group stared

at the closed door, they quickly realized that there was no handle on their side.

"Well, now look what you've done!" shouted Uncle Bert. "We're stuck here for good!"

"What *I've* done? You were holding the door, you great walrus!" retorted Reg. Lottie rolled her eyes at the bickering duo. She stepped in between them.

"Hush, you two!" she called. "Reg, you still have your crowbar. Can you open the door?"

Reg looked down to his belt, where he had casually stashed his crowbar. He handed Lottie his lamp and grumpily grabbed his crowbar as he pushed past Uncle Bert to get to the door. As he attacked it with the metal tool, Uncle

Bert paced uneasily a little farther down the tunnel.

Rumble.

"Honestly, Uncle Bert, you can't be hungry already. You've only just had breakfast," said Lottie.

Uncle Bert looked around to her.

"That . . . that wasn't my tummy, Lottie," he said with a look of fear. Lottie gulped.

RUMBLE!

"Then what—"

"*Cave-in!*" called Reg as he zoomed past them, grabbing Uncle Bert and Lottie's hands as he went. He ran so fast that Lottie thought he was going to pull her arm off. As he dragged them away from the door, Lottie saw the ceiling collapse and tons of earth and rubble come crashing down, filling the tunnel and blocking the door. Reg dived for cover, taking his friends with him. They landed in a heap on the ground, safe from the wreckage.

"All right," Reg puffed as he sat up, brushing the dust off his shirt. "I'll admit that this tunnel isn't *completely* safe."

With no choice but to press on forward and hope that the path would take them above ground at some point, Lottie and the two old men walked on. Lottie was glad to be heading toward the hoard of gold, but she would have been lying if she said that she

wasn't a little bit nervous. A collapsing tunnel wasn't her idea of fun.

After walking for what seemed like a very long time, the group came to what looked like a dead end. The tunnel simply stopped directly in front of them, and they were left staring at a wall.

"Now what?" said Uncle Bert, taking the lamp from Lottie and holding it up against the solid-looking wall. He was covered from head to toe in muck and puffing hard from walking so far. "We're stuck!"

"Hmm, not quite," said Reg. He looked down and cleared a pile of earth away with his foot, revealing a hole in the bottom of the wall, two small metal tracks, and a length of rope. "We used to do this in the mines. If we hit a wall of rock that was too tricky to get through, we'd clear a small tunnel and run a trolley through it."

Lottie bent down and pulled on the rope. A small wooden platform with wheels came  whizzing toward her. They would have to lie flat on the wooden platform and pull the rope by the side of them to get them through the tunnel.

"Pull ourselves through tons of rock? Not a chance!" said Uncle Bert.

"It'll be perfectly safe, I've done it loads of times . . ." Reg began to say. Lottie could feel their conversation was about to head into another argument. She looked down at the trolley. She really didn't fancy the trip either, but if their other choice was sitting in a tunnel and hoping to be rescued, then she knew what she had to do.

Without waiting for the two men to talk her out of it, she quickly lay on the trolley and pushed herself off through the narrow hole.

"Wheeeeeee!" she screamed as the trolley picked up speed. She didn't need to pull herself through with the rope as the track took her slightly downhill. She whizzed through

the tunnel, past hundreds of tons of rock and the entire city of London above her.

"Ooof!" She came to an abrupt stop in a large cavern. It seemed to be formed from a natural cave, and she rolled onto the stone floor, breathless with excitement.

"It's all right! It's safe! And quite fun!" she called up the small hole she had just come through. A tug on the rope sent the trolley back through the hole, and she was soon joined by a petrified-looking Uncle Bert and shortly after, Reg.

"Don't you ever do that again!" warned Uncle Bert, squeezing all of the air out of Lottie as he hugged her close to him. "Have you found a way out?"

"I've done better than that," said Lottie, pulling herself out of her Uncle Bert's grasp. She took the lamp from Uncle Bert and held it up, nodding to the wall in front of her. "I've found six."

The wall held six archways. Each was identical and too dark to see where they

led. There were carved symbols above each archway and something written in a strange language, chiseled into the stone above them:

OOKLAY OSERCLAY—OUYAY
AREWAY ETTINGGAY ARMWAY!

INDFAY EMAY UNDERWAY
AWAY OTHAY UNSAY!

"So which archway do we choose?" asked Reg.

"I don't know," said Uncle Bert. "But I can

imagine that five of them are filled with booby

traps. We had better choose wisely. Any ideas,

Lottie?"

But Lottie had no idea . . .

Can you crack
the code? Continue
reading to see if
you're right . . .

Lottie stared at the archways for a long time. The key had to be the language above the door. It looked familiar . . .

"Well, it certainly isn't English," said Uncle Bert. "Or Egyptian or Greek. If we're looking for Boudicca's hoard then I would have thought it would be in the language of the Romans, but it definitely isn't Latin."

Lottie looked over to Uncle Bert and smiled.

"That's it! Oh, Uncle Bert, I could kiss you!" she shrieked. "I knew I recognized that language!" She hurriedly reached for her trusty detective's notebook, where she kept all sorts of useful information. "It's not Latin, it's Pig Latin! A made-up language. All you do is take the first letter or two of the word and put it at the end, followed by 'ay.'"

Uncle Bert and Reg stared at her like she had lost her mind. Lottie ignored them and started scribbling down the translation in her notebook.

"'Ooklay' becomes 'look.' And 'oserclay' becomes . . . 'closer!' 'Look closer!'" Lottie said, starting to have fun. Within a minute she had written down the whole message:

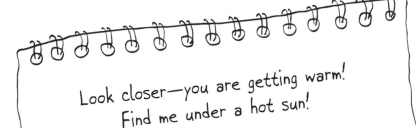

Look closer—you are getting warm!
Find me under a hot sun!

Lottie leaped up and marched through the archway with the sun above it.

"Lottie! Come back! It could be dangerous!" called Uncle Bert.

"It's fine!" said Lottie. "I'm just— *aaaggghhhhhh!*"

Chapter Four

For the second time that day, Lottie sank down a deep, dark hole and slid through a tunnel of smooth clay mud. If it hadn't been such a shock, she might have found it fun, but instead she screamed until her throat was sore.

"Aaaaaaaaaaaaaagggggggggggghhhhhhhhhh!"

Frantic thoughts whirred through her head. *Did I read the clue wrong? Maybe it was "snake" not "sun"? Where am I going to end up?*

Eventually she fell with a **PLOP** onto a muddy bank. She was still underground, but light was coming from high above. She was in a large cavern with a high ceiling and the sound of water rushing close by.

"Lottie!" came a call from the tunnel above her. "Are you okay?" It was Uncle Bert. Lottie stood and rubbed her bottom where she had plopped out onto the bank.

"I'm fine!" she called back up. "Come on down! It's quite safe, but a bit painful at the end."

She walked away from the tunnel and up to a small cliff in the cavern. Down below her she could see a river—the water was flowing

fast. It was lucky she hadn't fallen in there, or she would have been swept downstream in seconds.

"*Waaaaaaah!*" came a scream, followed by another. Uncle Bert and Reg plopped out onto the bank. They stood and brushed themselves down. They were both plastered from head to foot in mud.

"I'm getting too old for this," they both said in unison.

"Look, a river!" said Lottie. Uncle Bert joined her on the small cliff, which jutted out over the rushing water.

"Hmm. Must be the Walbrook. London has lots of underground rivers, most of which once flowed above ground but were covered over as the city grew larger. The Walbrook was an important river in Roman times, but it has gradually been forgotten about."

"Roman times? Then the hoard could be here!" said Lottie. She began to hunt around for a pile of glittering gold. Reg joined them and relit his mining lamp for Lottie. Shining it across the water, Lottie spotted what they had traveled so far to claim.

"Boudicca's hoard!" she squealed gleefully. "It really exists!"

Across the river on a piece of rock suspended above the fast-flowing water was a wooden chest. Directly opposite the chest, on Lottie's side of the water, was another piece of rock. She ran quickly over to the rock on her side. She could just walk out and grab the chest—it was that easy! She was about to step onto the ledge when a hand pulled her back.

"Now listen to me, Lottie Lipton," said Uncle Bert sternly. "I've said all along that this expedition was unsafe, but this *definitely* is not safe! Look!"

Looking closely, Lottie saw that her uncle was right. The chest wasn't on a ledge at all, but balanced on a flat rock, which was balancing over the river. Weighing down the flat rock on the bank opposite them were a

few rocks of different shapes. The hoard had been sitting there for thousands of years, with just a few lumps of stone to keep it from falling into the river.

Lottie then saw that the ledge she had been about to stand on was simply a flat rock, balanced carefully on the lip of the river bank. Just one little step on the rock and she would have sunk down into the river and been washed away underground into the River Thames. If she didn't drown first, of course . . .

"I hate to admit it, but your great uncle is right. We know where the hoard is now, so let's get out of here and come back later. I reckon I could reach that gap in the ceiling where the light is coming from. It probably leads to a drain somewhere," Reg said. The two men were about to turn back when Lottie spoke.

"We can't! If we don't get the hoard now, we won't have a home to go back to!"

She explained about overhearing Sir Trevelyan's conversation and how he needed a huge donation to keep the museum open. If they could get the hoard to him by the time the museum closed, they wouldn't lose the place they called home. Uncle Bert and

Reg took a few moments to think about it, then turned to each other and nodded.

"Let's get some treasure, then."

There were a lot of rocks lying around. Most were square in shape, but others were round. The square ones seemed to weigh twice as much as the round ones.

"We need to put some rocks on the end of this large stone to stop me from falling in," said Lottie, pointing at the stone balancing on the lip of the river bank.

They worked on finding the right balance by putting a round rock on one end and getting Lottie to lightly step on the other. If it teetered slightly, they put on another rock.

Eventually they worked out that Lottie weighed three round rocks. The treasure chest on the other side of the river was weighed down with two round rocks and one square rock.

"We've only got the heavier square rocks left," said Reg. "When you grab that chest, it'll weigh you down and you'll drop into the river."

Lottie gulped. She hadn't thought of that.

"If we put the rocks on now, the ledge will tilt upward, and you won't be able to reach the chest," said Uncle Bert.

Lottie took out her detective's notebook

and began to sketch out what they needed to
do to get across the water safely:

Can you work it
out? Read on
to see if you're
right . . .

"So we need to work out how many square rocks to put on this end of the stone at the exact same time that you grab the chest. Got it?"

Lottie wasn't sure she did "get it." She looked at the rushing river below them and hastily attempted to work out the right amount of square rocks. Time was ticking away, and she knew that they needed to return to the museum soon.

"Ooh, help!" she said in a tiny, desperate voice.

Lottie wasn't used to working with rocks and stones, but she was pretty good with numbers.

Just use numbers instead, she told herself. *If a round rock is worth one, then the square rocks are worth two. That means that I weigh three, and the chest weighs . . . four!*

She scribbled down another sketch to help her picture it:

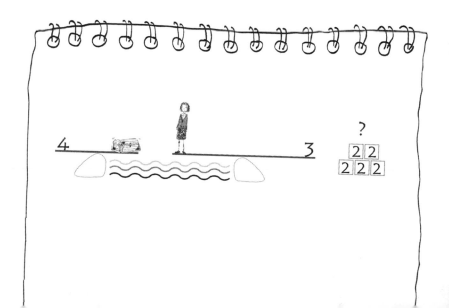

So when I pick up the chest, the combined weight of the chest and me will be seven. That means we need to add two square rocks onto the end of my stone to keep me from sinking into the water! Two plus two plus three equals seven! Yes!

"Two! It's two square rocks! I'm certain!" said Lottie, excited again. She showed Reg and Uncle Bert her notebook, and they nodded. With a deep breath, Lottie stepped onto the flat stone, which was already weighed down on the end resting on the river bank with three round rocks. It tipped a little, but Lottie stayed still, letting it settle. Slowly she edged to the end of the stone, toward to the river.

And there it was. Boudicca's hoard, balanced delicately on the end of its ledge. When Lottie reached out to grab it, she would be the first person in nearly two thousand years to touch it. She would also tip into the river if Reg and Uncle Bert didn't put the square rocks on at the right moment.

"Ready?" she called.

"Ready!" said the two men together. They each held a heavy rock, waiting to place it on the end of the tipping stone.

"Now!" Lottie yelled as she bent down, picking up the surprisingly heavy chest. Reg and Uncle Bert grunted, dropping the rocks down. Lottie let out a yelp as the stone

teetered, threatening to send her into the cold water below. It quickly leveled off, and Lottie stepped quickly but carefully over to safety.

"We did it!" she screamed with delight. They all hugged each other and looked up to the shaft of light above them. Lottie sighed, tired and relieved. "Gentlemen? Let's get out of here."

Chapter Five

Sir Trevelyan sat at the end of a long table. He looked tiny in the large boardroom, perched on his chair like a pixie. At the other end five men in suits and ties, each with a pair of half-moon glasses balanced on the ends of their noses, peered down the table. Lord Hart, the Chairman of the Board of Directors, cleared his throat.

"Ahem! Now, Sir Trevor—"

"Trevelyan," the curator corrected.

"Hmm? Ah yes. . . . This is not an easy decision, but as you know, donations to the museum have been rather thin on the ground as of late. Have you managed to collect any more?" Lord Hart asked.

Sir Trevelyan swallowed. He tried to speak, but he was so nervous that it came out as a whisper. "No, I haven't," he said quietly.

Lord Hart put his hand to his ear. "Pardon? Can you say that again?"

The door flung open behind Sir Trevelyan, and in walked Lottie, Reg, and Uncle Bert, out of breath and dripping with mud.

"He said yes!" Lottie shouted. "Sir Trevelyan

has managed to find a legendary historical artifact. And it's worth *thousands!*"

Sir Trevelyan looked horrified at the mud monsters behind him.

"I . . . I have?" he stuttered. Uncle Bert dropped the treasure chest on the table with a **THUNK**, and Reg gave the lock a hefty **THWACK** with his crowbar. The lid sprang open to reveal hundreds of golden coins, which spilled out onto the table. "I have!" he exclaimed.

Lottie gave him a wink.

"Goodness gracious!" Lord Hart cried. He rose from his seat and went to inspect the hoard. "How on Earth did you manage to lay your hands on this so quickly?" Sir Trevelyan was speechless for a moment. He looked back at the two men and the little girl who had saved his bacon and nodded to them. Lottie knew this meant "thank you." It was the kindest he had ever been to her.

"I had my best people on it," he said finally. Lottie smiled, and Reg went to shake his hand. "My best people, who really should go and take a bath."

After a quick spray-down with Reg's hose, Lottie was back in some fresh, mud-free clothes. She sat in her and Uncle Bert's untidy flat on the top floor of the museum. Uncle Bert arrived with two steaming hot cups of tea.

"There we are, my dear. Quite a day, hmm?" he said, sitting down next to her on the sofa and handing her some tea. "But there's one thing I can't figure out. Why did you say Sir Trevelyan had found the hoard?"

Lottie thought about it as she sipped her tea.

"Because even though he is sometimes beastly and rude to us, and tries to evict us at every opportunity, he loves the museum. It's his life, and I couldn't face taking that away from him. If Lord Hart knew he hadn't raised the money himself, he would have fired him. I didn't want that."

Uncle Bert smiled and kissed Lottie on the head.

"You, my dear, are an angel!"

Lottie smiled and hugged her great uncle.

"I know!" she laughed. She turned and kicked her feet over the back of the sofa so her head hung upside down, touching the floor. "Now if you'll excuse me, I have a crossword to finish . . ."

Glossary

archaeology: studying history by looking at old objects and ruins

catacombs: underground tunnels used as a cemetery

aureus: an ancient Roman coin

excavation: digging a hole to look at the objects or old ruins that have been buried over time

hoard: a collection of treasure

Latin: the language spoken by the ancient Romans

rebellion: when people come together to fight power

Did You Know?

- The Great Fire of London began in a bakery on Pudding Lane in 1666. It destroyed a large part of the city, including eighty-six churches and St. Paul's Cathedral.

- The ancient Romans built Londinium, where London stands today. Parts of the old city walls can still be seen.

- A statue of Boudicca, the Queen of the Iceni tribe who led an army against the Romans, can be found in London near the Palace of Westminster.

- Ancient Romans believed different gods and goddesses were in charge of different things. Neptune was the god of the sea, while Venus was the goddess of love.

Codebreaker

Use the mirror technique from Chapter One
to decipher this message:

You can use mirror writing to
make your own secret messages!
Try writing one here.

Escape the Catacombs!

Good news! You've found another hoard of gold!

Bad news! You're lost in the catacombs.

Can you find the right path to lead you out?